Thomas and the Bees
Reading Book

Illustrated by Niall Harding
Written by Brenda Apsley

Thomas the Tank Engine & Friends
A BRITT ALLCROFT COMPANY PRODUCTION
Based on The Railway Series by The Rev W Awdry
© Gullane (Thomas) LLC 2003

This pre-reading programme ...

is designed to encourage an early confidence in reading. It features the 45 frequent-use words as set out in the National Curriculum, plus key vocabulary from the Thomas Learning programme.

Listening to stories provides a very strong motivation for children to make the effort to learn to read themselves. Thomas and friends are well-loved characters. Children need exciting characters in stories so they will enjoy learning to read.

There is lots of repetition of key words and phrases. This encourages recognition of words and the link between their sounds and shapes. Your child will also begin to predict what is coming next, thus connecting written and spoken words, enabling them to 'read'.

To get the most out of the Look and Say books:

· read the stories several times with your child on different occasions;

· read the speech in a lively, animated style and point to the words;

· encourage your child to read aloud the words he/she has learned.

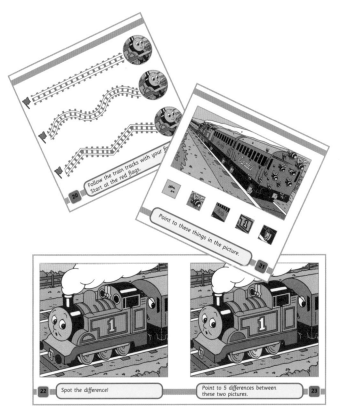

Other activities to enjoy

· **Follow the train tracks**

Children will trace with their finger from left to right in preparation for reading and writing.

· **Find the pictures**

Children will learn to observe small details In thls activity.

· **Spot the difference**

Children will compare two pictures - a skill used in reading when distinguishing letter shapes and words.

Thomas had two coaches called
Annie and Clarabel.

He liked them to go as fast as
they could.

"You are too slow, Annie,"
said Thomas. "Faster!"

6

"I'm going as fast as I can!"
said Annie.

"Hurry, Clarabel," said Thomas.
"Faster, faster!"

"I'm going as fast as I can!"
said Clarabel.

Some bees flew near Annie and Clarabel.

"Buzz, buzz," said the bees. "Hello."

"I do not like bees," said Annie.

"I do not like bees," said Clarabel.

Annie and Clarabel tried to get away
from the bees.

14

They went as fast as they could go.

"You are too slow, Thomas!" said Annie.

"Go faster, Thomas!" said Clarabel.

Thomas went as fast as he could go.
Now he was pleased.

18

"Peep!" he said. "I DO like bees!"

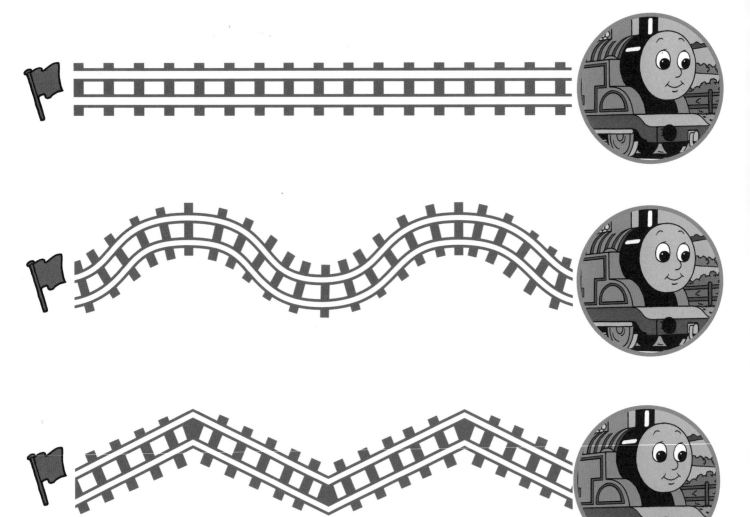

Follow the train tracks with your finger.
Start at the red flags.

Point to these things in the picture.

Spot the difference!

Point to 5 differences between these two pictures.

Thomas Reading

(age 4-6)

Develop your child's reading confidence with these six reading books, companion activity books and flash cards.

Thomas Maths

(age 4-6)

Introduce your child to early maths skills with these six maths story books, companion activity books and flash cards.